A focus on phonics helps beginning readers gain skill and confidence with reading. Each story in the Bright Owl Books series highlights one vowel sound—for *Princess Pig*, it's the short "i" sound. At the end of the book, you'll find three Story Starters, just for fun. Story Starters are open-ended questions that can be used as a jumping-off place for conversation, storytelling, and imaginative writing.

At Kane Press, we believe the most important part of any reading program is the shared experience of a good story. We hope you'll enjoy *Princess Pig* with a child you love!

For all bright-eyed, bright owl readers.

short **i**

Library of Congress Cataloging-in-Publication Data
Names: Coxe, Molly, author, illustrator.
Title: Princess pig / by Molly Coxe.
Description: First Kane Press edition. | New York : Kane Press, [2018] |
Series: Bright Owl Books | "Originally published in different form by BraveMouse Books in 2014"—Title page verso. | Summary: "Pig and Twig are playing princess, but even after Princess Pig has used her three wishes, she wants to make more"— Provided by publisher.
Identifiers: LCCN 2018007760 (print) | LCCN 2017038645 (ebook) | ISBN 9781575659800 (pbk) | ISBN 9781575659794 (pbk) | ISBN 9781575659787 (reinforced library binding) | ISBN 9781575659800 (ebook)
Subjects: | CYAC: Friendship—Fiction. | Pigs—Fiction. | Mice—Fiction. | Wishes—Fiction.
Classification: LCC PZ7.C839424 (print) | LCC PZ7.C839424 Pr 2018 (ebook) | DDC [E]—dc23
LC record available at https://lccn.loc.gov/2018007760

10 9 8 7 6 5 4 3 2 1

Printed in China

Book Design: Michelle Martinez

Bright Owl Books is a trademark of Kane Press, Inc.

Visit us online at
www.kanepress.com

Follow us on Twitter
@KanePress

Like us on Facebook
facebook.com/kanepress

Princess Pig

by Molly Coxe

Kane Press • New York

Pig and Twig
are playing princess.
"I'll be the princess," says Pig.
"Make three wishes," says Twig.

"I wish for lipstick!"
says Princess Pig.
"Swish! Wish!" says Twig.

"I wish for a picnic!"
says Princess Pig.
"Swish! Wish!" says Twig.

"I wish for kittens—
in mittens!"
says Princess Pig.
"Swish! Wish!"
says Twig.

"Now I will be the princess," says Twig.
"Not yet," says Princess Pig.
"I wish to make more wishes."

"I wish for nickels!"
says Princess Pig.
"Swish! Wish!" says Twig.

"I wish for pickles!"
says Princess Pig.
"Swish! Wish!" says Twig.

"I wish for sixteen pink popsicles!"
says Princess Pig.
"Swish! Wish!" says Twig.

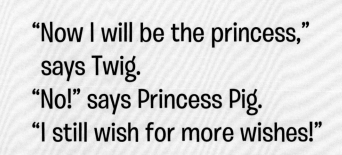

"Now I will be the princess,"
 says Twig.
"No!" says Princess Pig.
"I still wish for more wishes!"

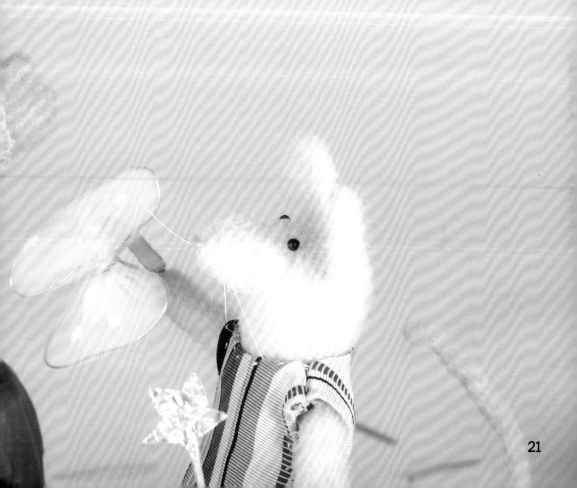

"No more wishes," says Twig.
"I quit!"

Pig misses Twig.

"Will you be the princess now?" asks Pig.
"Yippee!" says Twig.
"Make three wishes," says Pig.

"I wish to skip,

and sip,

and take a dip,
with my friend Pig!"

The End

Story Starters

Pig gives Twig another wish.
What will Twig wish?

37

Pig says,
"Swish! Wish! Make a wish!"
What will you wish?

Twig has a gift for Sis.
What is it?